MW00918273

If My Cat Could Fly

Written by A.J. Culey

Illustrated by Fabiana Farcas

Copyright © 2016 A.J. Culey

Print Edition

All rights reserved.

No part of this publication may be reproduced, distributed or transmitted,

in any form or by any means, or stored in a database or retrieval system

without the prior written permission of the publisher.

ISBN-13: 978-1536900149

ISBN-10: 1536900141

A POOF! Press Publication

If my cat could fly,
she would have
fairy wings.

She would fly to the top of the fridge

and to the rafters of the barn

and probably

she would fly right up

to the top

of my head

and sit there

and watch

the world.

If my cat could fly, she would fly

to the very top of the trees.

She would never need a firefighter
to save her again.

(That would be kind of sad for me.)

If my cat could fly, she would chase the birds all over the neighborhood.

Poor little birds.

They wouldn't be able to escape,

not even by flying away!

If my cat could fly,

she would fly to my rooftop

and stretch out in the sun.

She would pretend not to hear me

calling her for dinner

and not to see me

searching for her everywhere.

If my cat could fly, she would soar
to the highest shelves

and maybe break a thing or two.

If my cat could fly,

she'd lie in wait for me to come home.

She'd be so high, I wouldn't even see her, perched on the blade of a ceiling fan,

just waiting to pounce!

If my cat could fly,

I'd maybe be a little crazy,

wondering when

she'd jump

on my head next.

If my cat could fly,

she'd win every skirmish

with the dog

and the mailperson

and

the squirrels

and the

raccoons too!

If my cat could fly,

she'd maybe try and take over
the entire world!

If my cat could fly,

she'd still come home every night

and snuggle on my pillow,

nose in my ear,

tail wrapped under my chin,

wings brushing my cheek.

If my cat could fly,

she'd still be

my very best friend.

Thank you for reading

If My Cat Could Fly

* * *

Please consider leaving a review

on Amazon or Goodreads:

www.amazon.com/author/ajculey

www.goodreads.com/ajculey

* * *

If you would like to be notified of

upcoming new releases,

you may sign up at

www.ajculey.com/contact.html

Other books by A.J. Culey:

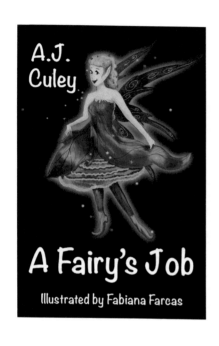

A Fairy's Job

Little Muffin Mae's just been elected this year's tooth fairy. The only problem? Every time Mae uses her magic, chaos results. The other fairies are pretty certain this year is going to be unforgettable.

Taco Runs Away

It's time for Taco's bath, but he'd rather have an adventure that doesn't involve water. Join Taco on his great escape.

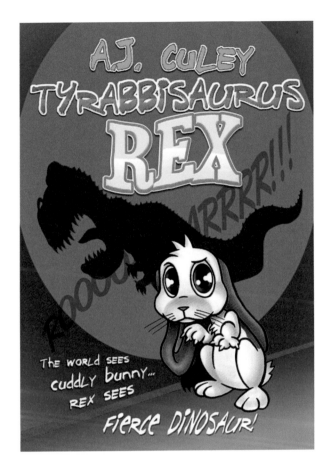

Tyrabbisaurus Rex

Tyrabbisaurus Rex doesn't appreciate being locked in a cage. Sure it has three levels and is full of scrumptious veggies, but that doesn't mean he's willing to accept his fate as a classroom pet.

Ginger's not happy about the always escaping, poopy rabbit. First, he chewed the dress her mom gave her. Now he keeps staring at her favorite hat. The demon bunny has got to go!

ABOUT THE AUTHOR

A.J. Culey is a teacher, world traveler and writer.

She lives with a number of very bossy cats.

Follow her:

www.ajculey.com

www.facebook.com/ajculey.author

www.twitter.com/ajculey

Follow T-Rab:

www.twitter.com/tyrabbisaurus

26530771R00015

Made in the USA
San Bernardino, CA
20 February 2019